Multiage class RM15

D1504589

THE LONG, BLUE BLAZER

A Beaver Book

Published by Arrow Books Limited
62-65 Chandos Place, London WC2N 4NW

An imprint of Century Hutchinson Ltd

London Melbourne Sydney Auckland
Johannesburg and agencies throughout the world

First published by Andersen Press in 1987

Beaver edition 1989

Text © 1987 by Jeanne Willis
Illustrations © 1987 by Susan Varley

Printed in Italy by Grafiche AZ, Verona

ISBN 0 09 958680 0

THE LONG, BLUE BLAZER

Jeanne Willis · Susan Varley

Beaver Books

When I was five, there was a boy in my class who wore a long, blue blazer. He had short arms and short legs and big feet that stuck out from under his long, blue blazer.

He arrived one winter's day. He wandered into the classroom covered in snow and shook hands with the teacher. She said, "You must be Wilson, the new boy."

She told him to hang up his things. He took off his cap and his scarf and his mittens. But he wouldn't take off his long, blue blazer.

The teacher asked him to, but he said he was cold, so she let him keep it on.

Later on we did some painting. We all had to put plastic aprons on, but Wilson put his apron on over his long, blue blazer.

I painted my mum in a pink, flowery dress and Mary painted her mum in green stripy trousers. But Wilson painted his mum in a long, blue blazer.

He ate his school dinner in his long, blue blazer. He did his sums in his long, blue blazer. He even did P.E. in his long, blue blazer.

The teacher asked him to take it off, but he said his mother would be angry if he did, so she let him keep it on.

When it was time to go home, my mum came
to fetch me, but nobody came for Wilson.
He stood alone in his long, blue blazer,
staring up at the sky. The teacher asked him
why his mother hadn't come to fetch him. He
said she lived too far away.

Wilson walked slowly through the schoolgates, his long, blue blazer dragging in the snow.

The teacher spoke to my mum and I was told to run after Wilson and invite him for tea.

That seemed to make him happy. But when my mum asked him to take off his long, blue blazer, he looked as if he was about to cry, so she let him keep it on.

She gave him some steak and kidney pie and sat him on her lap. He put his arms round her and started to cry. He said he was tired.

Mum carried Wilson up to my bedroom and sat him on a chair while she fetched him some pyjamas. When she came back, he'd climbed into my bunkbed in his long, blue blazer and pulled the blankets around him. I slept in the bottom bunk.

Later that night, a loud humming noise woke me up. The wind was making the curtains flap, so I got up to shut the window. I saw green and yellow flashing lights, and there, standing on the windowsill, was Wilson. Suddenly . . . he jumped.

The last I ever saw of him was his long, blue TAIL!

Other titles in the Beaver/Sparrow Picture Book series: